After HAPPILY —EVER— AFTER

Cinderella and the
Mean Queen

After Happily Ever After was published in the United States
in 2009 and 2014 by Stone Arch Books, A Capstone Imprint
1710 Roe Crest Drive, North Mankato, Minnesota 56003
www.capstoneyoungreaders.com

First published by Orchard Books, a division of Hachette Children's Books
338 Euston Road, London NW1 3BH, United Kingdom

Library of Congress Cataloging-in-Publication Data is available
on the Library of Congress website.

ISBN: 978-1-4342-7960-6 (paperback)

Summary: Cinderella's Prince Charming is just perfect, but his mother
is a royal pain. She makes the ugly stepsisters look friendly! With a little
makeover magic, Cinderella is ready to turn the Mean Queen into the
Nice Queen.

Designer: Russell Griesmer
Photo Credits: ShutterStock/Maaike Boot, 5, 6, 7, 54-55

Printed in China.
092013   007737LEOS14

After HAPPILY —EVER— AFTER

Cinderella and the Mean Queen

by TONY BRADMAN
illustrated by SARAH WARBURTON

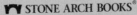
STONE ARCH BOOKS®
a capstone imprint

TABLE OF CONTENTS

So Cinderella and Prince Charming were married and lived happily ever after. And then ...

CHAPTER ONE

"Hurry up, Cinderella," said her husband, Prince Charming. "You know Mother hates it when we're late for dinner."

"Coming, sweetheart," Cinderella
murmured. She checked herself one
last time in her full-length mirror.

"What do you think of this dress and these boots?" she asked. "I'm trying out a new style."

"They're fine," the prince said. "Can we go now?"

Cinderella sighed. She loved the prince, and he loved her. She'd thought her troubles would be over when they got married.

But it was hard living with Prince Charming's parents in the castle. Everything was so fancy. She missed the little cottage where she had lived with her father.

Sometimes she even missed her Wicked Stepmother and the Ugly Sisters. They didn't seem too bad when she thought about them now. At least not compared to Prince Charming's mother, the queen.

"And WHERE have you two been?" the
queen roared as the prince and Cinderella
entered the royal dining room. "Your soup
is getting cold!"

"Sorry, Mother," said the prince.

"You look lovely this evening, my dear," said the king, smiling at Cinderella. He was always very sweet to her.

"You never compliment me," snapped
the queen. The king opened his mouth
to speak, but the queen held up her
spoon and glared.

"Don't bother. I know I look dreadful these days," the queen went on. "But I can't spend all day making myself look pretty. I have more important things to do!"

Cinderella had a feeling the queen would like the king to pay her compliments. She had seen the queen glancing at herself in mirrors. Then she would sigh and frown.

CHAPTER TWO

The queen was really mean to Cinderella that evening. Later, Cinderella sat at her dressing table and cried. The Prince put his arm around her.

"Don't let her upset you, Cinders," he said softly, passing her a royal hankie. "I'm certain Mother likes you. Deep down, anyway."

"No, she doesn't," Cinderella wailed.

"She hates me. I've heard her saying I'm useless, and I'm only here because of the Fairy Godmother. Well, I've had enough. I'll prove to her that I'm not just a pretty face."

"Really?" said the prince. "What do you have in mind?"

"I'm going to get a job," said Cinderella. "A good one, too."

"Gosh!" said the prince, his eyes wide. "I'm impressed already!"

CHAPTER THREE

In the morning, Cinderella looked
in the paper. She soon found a job
opening. Fairy Tale Fashions, the best
clothing store in the forest, was looking
for a salesperson.

Cinderella had liked clothes and fashion ever since her own transformation. She often looked at other people and thought she might be able to help them. Maybe give them some advice on how to improve their styles.

She called for an application. When it
arrived, she quickly filled it out, sent it
back, and waited nervously. Her phone
rang the next day.

"Oh hi, yes, this is Cinderella Charming," she said. "I got the job? Wow, fantastic! But wait, aren't you going to interview me or anything? You're not, I see. When do I start? Nine o'clock tomorrow? Okay."

Cinderella was surprised it had been so easy. Surely it should have been harder. After all, she'd never had a real job before. Then she shrugged and started choosing an outfit to wear.

The prince insisted on taking her to
work in the royal coach. But when
they arrived, things weren't quite what
Cinderella had expected.

The royal guards had to hold back a large crowd. Wild cheering broke out as Cinderella walked up the red carpet that led to the store's entrance.

The manager and staff of Fairy Tale
Fashions were there to greet her.

"I don't understand," said Cinderella.
"What are all these people doing here?
I didn't think your big sale started for
another couple of months?"

"They're here to see you, Your Highness," said the manager, curtseying. "What a story! Rags to riches, a grand ball, midnight, the glass slipper — it's all so romantic! Now, there's a TV news crew waiting."

Cinderella's heart sank. She realized Fairy Tale Fashions didn't have a real job for her. They just wanted to use her for publicity. She let the TV crew film her. Then she signed autographs.

Then she got in the royal carriage and
went home. She ran up to her room
and burst into tears.

After dinner that evening, the royal
family watched the news. The queen was
even meaner than before.

"What a complete waste of time."
Cinderella heard her say. "She'll never
amount to anything. Plus, she's not
even that pretty."

Cinderella didn't go back to Fairy
Tale Fashions. She called them the next
morning and quit.

Cinderella went for a long walk in the royal gardens. She wondered what she should do. Perhaps she could apply for another job. But the same thing would probably happen again. After all, everybody knew her name and her story.

Cinderella was so fed up! She even
thought about trying to get in touch with
her Fairy Godmother. But she realized
that would only prove the queen was
right about her.

Whatever she did, she would have to do
it without any help. Then Cinderella had
an idea.

She spent the rest of that week
planning. She surfed the Forest Web
to see if she had any competition. But
nobody else seemed to be doing what
she had in mind.

CHAPTER FOUR

A month later, she started her business, Cinderella Makeover Limited. She had a big party in the royal ballroom. Lots of people were invited, and the event was covered by Forest TV and all the newspapers.

"They're only interested because she's one of us," the queen said snootily. But Cinderella didn't have time to worry. She was too busy showing everyone what she could do.

A couple of people at the party wanted to be transformed. The results were amazing.

"Wow!" said Little Red Riding Hood's granny when she saw herself.

"I love the way you've done my hair, and these clothes are fantastic! I look at least 20 years younger. I can't thank you enough!"

The queen didn't say a word. She did
seem impressed, though.

Soon Cinderella had lots of clients. She worked her magic on every witch in the forest, several trolls, and the Bad Fairy. Not to mention dozens of wicked stepmothers, including her own, who turned up one day with the Ugly Sisters.

If I can help those three out, I can do anything! thought Cinderella.

It was a real success. It even led to her
getting her own series on Forest TV,
The Cinders Show.

The Wicked Stepmother and the Ugly
Sisters were very grateful. They begged
Cinderella to forgive them for being
horrible to her in the past. Cinderella
did, and from that day on they were
great friends.

CHAPTER FIVE

Not long after that, somebody else came to see Cinderella in her salon. It was the queen. She came in, sat down, and smiled nervously.

"I know I haven't been the best mother-in-law to you, Cinderella," she said. "But I've seen your show on television, and I just wondered ..."

Cinderella smiled and got straight to work. She tackled the queen's hair, makeup, and clothes. This time she outdid herself.

That evening, Cinderella and the queen walked into the royal dining room together. The prince and the king were shocked.

"My goodness!" said the king at last, staring at his wife. His eyes were misty with admiration and love. "You look absolutely stunning, dear!"

The queen was delighted, and so was Prince Charming.

"Well done, Cinders!" he said as he kissed her.

And so Cinderella, Prince Charming, his parents, and everyone else in the forest who needed fashion and beauty advice lived happily ever after!

ABOUT THE AUTHOR

Tony Bradman writes for children of all ages. He is particularly well known for his top-selling Dilly the Dinosaur series. His other titles include the Happily Ever After series, *The Orchard Book of Heroes and Villains*, and *The Orchard Book of Swords, Sorcerers*, and *Superheroes*. Tony lives in South East London.

ABOUT THE ILLUSTRATOR

Sarah Warburton is a rising star in children's books. She is the llustrator of the Rumblewick series, which has been very well received at an international level. The series spans across both picture books and fiction. She has also illustrated nonfiction titles and the Happily Ever After series. She lives in Bristol, England, with her young baby and husband.